D1128486

Books by Janice May Udry
published by
Albert Whitman & Company

ALFRED
END OF THE LINE
BETSY-BACK-IN-BED

Next Door to Laura Linda

JANICE MAY UDRY

Pictures by

MEG WOHLBERG

ALBERT WHITMAN & COMPANY Chicago

J
Udry

L.C. Catalog Card Number: 65-15105
Published simultaneously in Canada by George J. McLeod, Ltd., Toronto
Lithographed in the U.S.A.

Poor Laura Linda Tucker!
Almost nothing was the way
she wanted it to be.

She had blue eyes.
"I wish they were brown,"
said Laura Linda.

She had yellow brown hair.
"I wish it was brownish black,"
said Laura Linda.

She had a big brother.
"I wish I had a baby sister,"
said Laura Linda.

She had a swing in a tree.
"I wish I had a tree house,"
said Laura Linda.

She lived in a pink house.
"I wish it was yellow,"
said Laura Linda.

Worst of all,
the yellow house
next door to Laura Linda's
was empty.

"I wish a little girl
lived there," she said.
"I wish a little girl
with brown eyes
and brownish black hair
lived there who had
a baby sister
and a tree house."

Laura Linda often wished that
lots of things were different.
But half the summer went by
and nothing changed.

Laura Linda still had blue eyes,
yellow brown hair, a big brother,
a swing in a tree, and a pink house.

The house next door was still empty.

Then one day a big truck rolled up
to the house next door,
and the men carried in rugs
and furniture.
The house next door was
no longer empty.

"I hope there's a little girl,
I hope there's a little girl,
I *hope* there's a little girl,"
said Laura Linda Tucker over and over.

She couldn't see over the hedge
and her mother told her
not to go next door.

So Laura Linda swung higher
and higher and higher until
she could see over the hedge.

She saw a mother and a father.
She saw a baby buggy.
That was all.
"No little girl,"
said Laura Linda sadly.
"No one for me to play with."

Poor Laura Linda Tucker!
Almost nothing was the way
she wanted it to be.

There was nothing to do
except sit in her swing
and wind herself up,
let herself go,
and spin around
very, very fast
until she was dizzy.

"Hey! What are you doing?"
asked a voice.

Laura Linda looked around,
but she couldn't see anyone.
She was very dizzy.
She had wound herself up
for the fifth time.
"Where are you?"
she asked the voice.

"Up here," said the voice.
"Is that fun?"

"Is what fun?" asked Laura Linda,
still looking around.

"Winding yourself up in a swing
like that," said the voice.

"It's fun," said Laura Linda,
"if you like to get dizzy.
I think a tree house would be more fun.
Say, where are you?"

"Up here—in the tree—making a tree house.
I didn't have any rope to make a swing
so I'm making a tree house.
I have a lot of boards and boxes
from the moving."

Then Laura Linda saw a boy in the tree
just on the other side of the hedge.
"Are you coming down?" asked Laura
Linda.
"Can you come over?"

"Sure," answered the boy.
And he scrambled down the tree—

and popped through the hedge.
"My name is Spencer," he said.
"I'm Laura Linda," said Laura Linda.

Spencer had brown eyes
and brownish black hair.
"Have you got a baby sister?"
asked Laura Linda.
"Yes, I have. She's really little.
How did you know?" asked Spencer.
"I saw the baby buggy," said Laura Linda.
"I've got a big brother."

"Can I swing?" asked Spencer.

"Yes," said Laura Linda.
"Can I go up in your tree house?"

"Yes," said Spencer.
"I was wishing a boy my age
lived here when I saw the swing.
But I don't mind that you're a girl."

"And I was wishing a girl my age
would move next door," said Laura Linda.
"But I don't mind that you're a boy.
You do have brown eyes,
brownish black hair,
a baby sister,
a yellow house,
and a tree house.
So you're almost as good."

Laura Linda and Spencer played so much
through all the long summer days that
Laura Linda never had time to wish
that things were different anymore.

Anyway—she liked the way things were!